La Princesa and the Pea

SUSAN MIDDLETON ELYA

illustrated by
JUANA MARTINEZ-NEAL

G. P. PUTNAM'S SONS

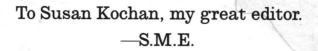

To Susan Kochan, my great editor.
—S.M.E.

To all the moms who want the best for their boys,
and all the boys who know what is best for them.
And, to Chris.
—J.M-N.

Glossary

acepto [*ah SEHP toe*] I do

(el) **anillo** [*ah NEE yoe*] ring

ay [*I*] oh my

(la) **boca** [*BOE kah*] mouth

(la) **boda** [*BOE dah*] wedding

(las) **bombones** [*bome BOE nehs*] candies

(los) **brazos** [*BRAH soce*] arms

buena [*BWEH nah*] good

(la) **cama** [*KAH mah*] bed

(el) **castillo** [*kahs TEE yoe*] castle

(los) **colchones** [*kole CHOE nehs*] mattresses

cuatro [*KWAH troe*] four

de moda [*DEH MOE dah*] in style

dos [*DOSE*] two

el, los [*EHL, LOS*] the (masculine singular and plural)

en la cama [*EHN LAH KAH mah*] in the bed

gris [*GREECE*] gray

(el) **guisante** [*ghee SAHN teh*] pea

(los) **hijos** [*EE hoce*] children

(el) **jardín** [*hahr DEEN*] garden

la, las [*LAH, LAHS*] the (feminine singular and plural)

(la) **madre** [*MAH dreh*] mother

mamá [*mah MAH*] momma

muy grande [*MWEE GRAHN deh*] very big

(la) **niña** [*NEE nyah*] girl

(los) **ojos** [*OE hoce*] eyes

pequeño [*peh KEH nyoe*] small

pobrecita [*poe breh SEE tah*] poor thing

(la) **princesa** [*preen SEH sah*] princess

(el) **príncipe** [*PREEN see peh*] prince

(la) **reina** [*RRAY nah*] queen

(la) **roca** [*RROE kah*] rock

suave [*SWAH veh*] soft

tres [*TREHS*] three

uno [*OO noe*] one

un sueño [*OON SWEH nyoe*] a dream

veinte [*VAYN teh*] twenty

There once was a prince who wanted a wife.
But not any *niña* would do in his life.

His *madre* was picky. She hoped for perfection.

The prince was so lonely—in need of affection.

But here came a maiden, en route to her castle.
"I hope I can stay here, if it's not a hassle."

She winked at the prince, who fell for her fast.
No matter what Mom does, I'll marry this lass!

The prince said, "Come in," but his mother, *la reina*, decided to test her. Would this girl be *buena*?

Mamá sneaked away
to the royal jardín
and found a small pea
that was fit for a queen.

She guarded the pea pod and took to the stair.

"If this girl is worthy, she'll feel that it's there."

She placed **el guisante** in the bed for their guest.
She yelled, "*VEINTE* mattresses!" (Lofty request.)

The queen settled in with her box of **bombones**,
while lots of strong workers came in with **colchones**.

Uno was *suave*, *dos* was *pequeño*,
tres was *muy grande*, *cuatro—un sueño*.

Several were pin-striped, some made of fleece;
others were dotted or checkered or *gris*.

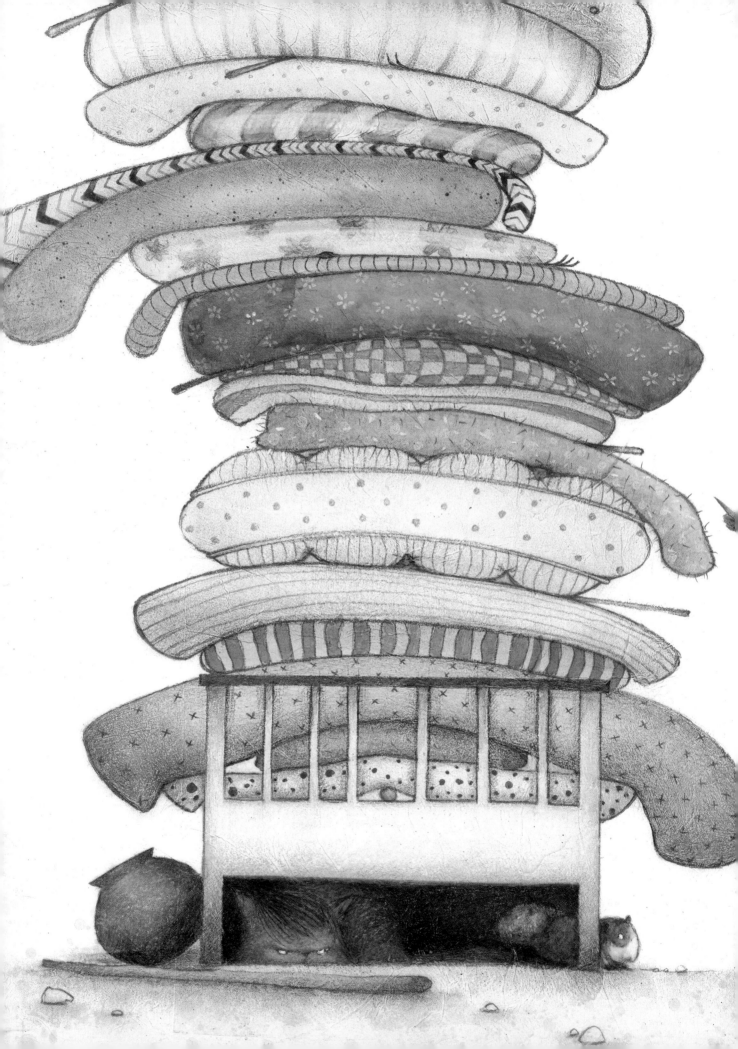

The queen ate her treats. The bed was stacked high,
and right when they finished, la niña came by.

"Here is your cama, a place you can sleep."
"Thanks!" said the girl. "I won't even count sheep."

Meanwhile, *el príncipe* practiced I do's.

He knew that this maiden was one he should choose.

"I like her, *Mamá*," he said with a lilt.

"We'll see," said the queen as she fluffed up his quilt.

The girl stretched her *brazos*
and yawned with her *boca*.
But the bed felt so lumpy,
like there was a *roca*.

The little *guisante*
was twenty times deep.
Could it be the reason
the girl got no sleep?

She trudged down to breakfast, her *ojos* so droopy.
"And how was your slumber?" *La reina* was snoopy.

"Great," said the girl, "if you like hard and lumpy."
"Oh, *pobrecita!*" the prince said. "You're grumpy!"

Their guest brightened up as she noticed the lad.
"Really," she murmured, "it wasn't that bad."

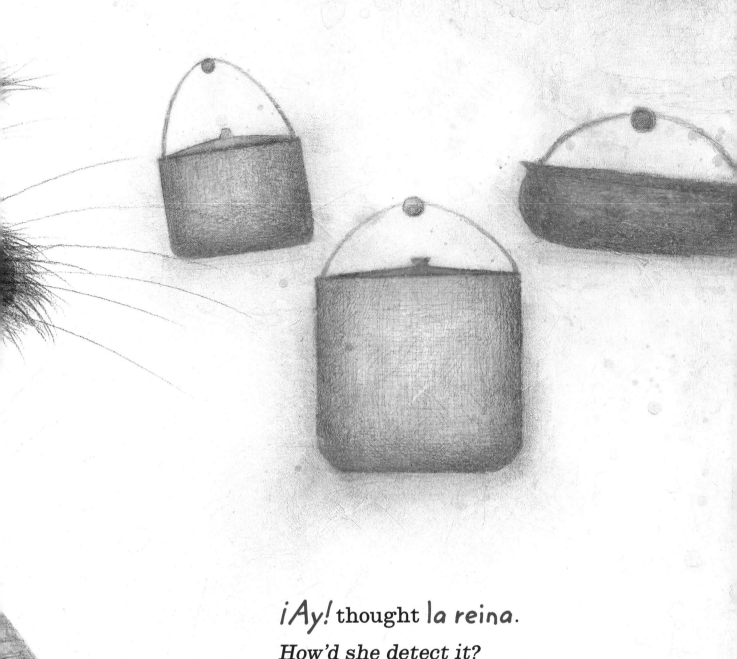

¡Ay! thought *la reina.*
How'd she detect it?
Is she a real princess?
I think I suspect it.

She signaled her son
that the girl passed the test.
"Drat!" She had managed
to stave off the rest.

The prince soon proposed with a golden *anillo*.
They married that week in the royal *castillo*.

The queen kept her promise and threw a big *boda*.
The bride wore a wedding gown, stylish—*de moda*.

¡Acepto! ¡Acepto! They both said, "I do."
And still, to this day, the queen has no clue...

The prince had put pitchforks and stones *en la cama*,
to help his true love pass the test of Queen Momma.

The prince and his bride had *hijos* galore,
one for each mattress, and then had no more.

A Note from the Illustrator

The textiles in this book were inspired by the weaving and embroidery of indigenous people of Peru. The villagers of Huilloc, in the mountains of the province of Cusco, weave alpaca wool into clothing and blankets similar to those seen on *el príncipe* and *la reina* and in their home. *La princesa*'s embroidered clothing was inspired by the people of the Colca Canyon in the province of Arequipa. The methods and traditions of dyeing, spinning, weaving, and embroidery have been passed down from generation to generation, and their remote locations have kept these communities distinct. I traveled to Huilloc and Colca Canyon for the first time with my father. I hope to encourage you, the readers, to value and protect these groups so they can maintain their culture and traditions and continue to thrive in the future. —Juana Martinez-Neal

G. P. PUTNAM'S SONS
an imprint of Penguin Random House LLC
375 Hudson Street
New York, NY 10014

Text copyright © 2017 by Susan Middleton Elya. Illustrations copyright © 2017 by Juana Martinez-Neal.

G. P. Putnam's Sons is a registered trademark of Penguin Random House LLC.

Library of Congress Cataloging-in-Publication Data

Names: Elya, Susan Middleton, 1955– author. | Martinez-Neal, Juana, illustrator. | Andersen, H. C. (Hans Christian), 1805–1875. Prindsessen paa µrten. | Title: La princesa and the pea / Susan Middleton Elya ; illustrated by Juana Martinez-Neal. Description: New York, NY : G. P. Putnam's Sons, [2017] | Summary: "A rhyming twist on a classic fairy tale in which a queen places a pea under a young lady's mattress to see if she is truly a princess. Incorporates Spanish words and includes a glossary"—Provided by publisher. | Identifiers: LCCN 2016017143 | ISBN 9780399251566 (hardcover) Subjects: | CYAC: Stories in rhyme. | Fairy tales. | Spanish language—Vocabulary. Classification: LCC PZ8.3.E514 Pr 2017 | DDC [E]—dc23 | LC record available at https://lccn.loc.gov/2016017143

Manufactured in China by RR Donnelley Asia Printing Solutions Ltd.
ISBN 9780399251566
3 5 7 9 10 8 6 4

Book design and title lettering by Jaclyn Reyes.
Text set in New Clarendon.
The art was created with acrylics, colored pencils
and graphite on handmade textured paper.